BOOK 1

Cole's Perfect Puppy

By

Frances M. Crossno

Cole's Perfect Puppy
Perfect Puppies Series Book One
Copyright ©2016 Frances M. Crossno

ISBN 978-1506-901-68-8 PRINT
ISBN 978-1506-901-69-5 EBOOK

LCCN 2016935061

February 2016

Published and Distributed by
First Edition Design Publishing, Inc.
P.O. Box 20217, Sarasota, FL 34276-3217
www.firsteditiondesignpublishing.com

Library of Congress Cataloging-in-Publication Data
Crossno, Frances M.
  Cole's Perfect Puppy / written by Frances M. Crossno.
  p. cm.
  ISBN 978-1506-901-68-8 pbk, 978-1506-901-69-5 digital

1. JUVENILE FICTION/General. 2. /Animals/Dogs. 3. /Religious/Christian/Early Readers.

C6937

Table of Contents

Chapter 1

The Dog House

"Hurry up and pick one, Caleb! Uncle Bobby wants us to be home before dark. And I want to go to the Dog House before we go home." I sat my backpack down and looked at the clock behind the counter.

It was 4:45 and I knew it would be dark by 5:30. It always gets dark early in the winter time – especially this close to Christmas. I figured it would take us thirty minutes to get back to our bikes and ride home from the mall. That would leave only fifteen minutes to play with the puppies at the pet store – if we hurried.

Caleb looked up from the video games he was holding. "Cole," he said, "I like both of these games, but I only have money for one. Which one do you think has the most action?"

I groaned and grabbed the games. I like video games too, but I really wanted to go play with the puppies. It was my last chance before Christmas. "Here, this one," I said and shoved the new 'Truck Trauma' game at him. I put the other game back on the shelf. "Go pay for it and let's go."

"Okay," he said. He fumbled with his backpack and pulled out an old bank bag Uncle Bobby let him use to carry his coins.

I groaned again. It was going to take a long time to count out the coins. I picked up my backpack and thought about going on ahead. The pet store was only a couple of stores down. But I wasn't supposed to leave my younger brother by himself at the mall. I went to the door and looked out while I waited. I made sure I could still see Caleb from where I stood.

Oh, no! There was a crowd of people at the Dog House. Families with children were standing around the display window looking at the puppies. I could also see a crowd of people inside the store. I would not have time to get any of the puppies out of the cages to play. My heart sank.

"I'm ready," Caleb said. His game was in a shopping bag and he had a big smile on his face.

I felt a little bad about rushing him. I just had to look at the puppies, even if there wasn't time to play with them. I took a last look at the clock behind the counter. It was 5:00 - time to leave for home. I grabbed Caleb's hand. "Come on."

I pushed through the now large crowd at the window of the Dog House, pulling Caleb with me. "Excuse, me," I said to the man I nudged out of the way. I knew Mom would not have approved, but I would worry about that later.

Suddenly, I was right up to the window. There they were!

All thoughts of heading home, of taking care of Caleb, of Mom and Dad being gone at Christmas - just flew out of my head.

A big puppy, with thick, gray and silver fur, shook a ball at the other puppies. A solid-black puppy ran around the big one and nipped at his heels. A white puppy with black spots growled at a brown, wrinkled puppy. It was funny to see wrinkles on a puppy.

"Look at that one!" Caleb said, pointing to a little puppy with red-golden fur. She was jumping on the window, trying to lick a man's hand. The puppy couldn't understand why she couldn't lick his fingers through the glass. She sat down with a thud and a single frustrated bark.

I have heard grown-ups talk about 'love' at first sight. Until now, I never really understood what they meant. But there she was. The love of my life!

Chapter 2
The Chase

I couldn't believe my luck. The manager of the Dog House opened the back of the display window and picked up the red-golden pup. He put her on the floor. The crowd moved back a little to give the puppy room.

Caleb and I pushed our way inside. The puppy sniffed around the floor and pawed at the top of the manager's shoes.

"Let me see her," said a teenage girl at the front of the crowd. She picked up the puppy. The pup wiggled and licked the girl's fingers. Several girls closed in around them, all trying to pet the puppy at once.

"Oh, she is so cute!" said another girl in a green sweater with a Santa face on the front. "Let me hold her next," she said.

I tried to get closer but there were too many girls. I checked to make sure Caleb was still behind me and then moved to the other side of the crowd.

Caleb pushed past a lady carrying a big red purse to stand beside me. He was holding tightly to the bag with his video game.

The little red-golden puppy was passed from one girl to the next until one of them cried, "Oh, no. The puppy tore a hole in my sweater!" She dropped the puppy back to the floor.

I heard little nails scrambling on the tile but couldn't see where she went. The manager was yelling. "Oh, my! There she goes! Somebody catch her before she gets out of the shop!"

The lady with the big purse dropped it and bent down, spreading out her arms.

I heard the scrambling sound again and felt something move between my legs. By the time I got down on my knees, all I could see was a fluffy red tail wagging between a tall man's legs. I watched the tail move quickly around the lady with the purse and out into the crowded, busy mall.

I looked at Caleb. He was grinning because he knew what I was thinking. We are a lot faster than all of the adults in the store. "Let's go," I whispered. The chase was on!

The puppy was fast. She knocked packages from the hands of shoppers all the way down the hall. By the time they knew what happened, she was long past them. It was all Caleb and I could do to keep from running into people as we chased the red tail.

When we lost sight of the tail, we followed her by the sounds of disturbed packages and the shouts of surprised shoppers.

We rounded a corner and headed down another wing of the mall. I heard shouts and footsteps far behind us. The pet store manager was surely among them, as I heard him shouting, "Catch her! Catch her!" He was breathing hard.

So were we. I dropped my backpack as we ran on. I would go back to get it later.

Ahead, I could see something new was happening. A red-golden ball of fur was tugging on a bright-blue ribbon sticking out of a shopping bag. A young man tugged back.

"Let go! Let go, you little thief!" he yelled.

Soon the red fur ball was trailing a bright-blue roll of ribbon behind her, as she continued running down the hall.

I saw a young man in a security guard uniform come out of a store we ran past. He soon caught up with us.

I stopped to catch my breath and Caleb ran into me, causing us both to fall down.

The guard stopped too. He held out his hands to help us up. "What is going on?" he asked, as I brushed off my jeans.

I was still breathing hard. I pointed in the direction I last saw the pretty red tail. "Uh...puppy...loose!" I managed to say.

By this time, some of the other chasers were running past us. I grabbed Caleb's hand. "Come on," I said. "I want to be the one to catch her."

We ran even faster to get back in front. I took a quick look behind. The security guard was trying to catch up.

The chase merged into the crowd at a big department store at the end of the hall. I stopped. I couldn't see where the puppy was.

"Cole, I'm too tired to run anymore," Caleb said. His face was red, and he was breathing hard when he caught up with me.

I put my hands on my knees and looked behind us. There weren't as many people following us as before. The store manager still followed but at walking speed now. The security guard was almost up with us, though.

CRASH!

A stream of silver and red Christmas balls rolled around us. Up ahead, I could hear both barking and yelling. The security guard went past us. The barking turned into howling.

"Whooooooo! Whoooooooo!"

I shook my head at Caleb. I couldn't run any more either. The crowd closed in front of us. All I could see was a mass of people hovered around what once had been a beautiful holiday display.

"I got her!" It was the security guard's voice. That was soon followed by, "Ow! Her little teeth are sharp!"

The crowd stirred. The puppy was loose again and heading back in our direction.

I stood still. A little red-golden fur ball collided with my leg. She paused and then sat down right on my foot. She looked up at me with big, brown eyes and howled. "Whooooo! Whooooo!"

I picked her up and held her close to my face. She stopped howling and licked my face all over. I held her up, so I could see her better. She stuck out her tongue, panting. She was out of breath too, but her shining eyes said it all. "Isn't this fun? I could do it again real soon!" A bit of stolen blue ribbon still clung to her collar. She had stolen the ribbon and my heart as well!

I pulled her down on my chest and held her close. As the crowd closed in around us, I glanced at the skylight. It was completely dark outside.

Chapter 3

Rachel

"Was Uncle Bobby mad when you called him?" Caleb asked.

"He was mostly happy to get my call," I replied, as we left the mall office. "He said I did the right thing to call him to come get us, instead of going home in the dark. It's dangerous to ride our bikes at night. People driving cars might not see us on the road."

I pointed toward the center of the mall. "Uncle Bobby said we should go to the food court and wait for him there. He'll put our bikes in the back of his SUV."

"There's an empty table over there." Caleb pointed. It was even more crowded in the mall than before, as people came after work to shop for Christmas presents.

"Let's grab it!" I said.

We hurried through the people but someone else beat us to the table. We looked around for another one. All the tables were full. "Watch for someone who is getting ready to leave," I told Caleb.

We waited for a few minutes. "Hey, the girl over there is waving for us to come over." I pointed to the girl in a faded red sweater near the cookie booth. She continued to wave and point to the empty chairs at her table.

Caleb looked, and then groaned. "I don't want to sit with her!"

"Why not? Isn't she in your class at school?"

"Yes. That is wrinkled Rachel," he whined.

"Wrinkled Rachel?"

"That is what the boys call her. Her clothes are always wrinkled like they were crumpled up in the dryer for a long time. I don't want anyone to see us with her."

"Caleb! You know it's wrong to call someone names. Even if her clothes are wrinkled or you don't like her."

"I didn't call her that. Tony Marshal did. I mostly just stay away from her. After all, she is a girl."

"Well, you should tell Tony not to call her names. It's hurtful. It might make Tony feel important but it really just makes him mean." I looked back at the girl. She pointed again to the chairs. "Come on. I don't care if her sweater is wrinkled. This backpack is getting heavy."

"Oh, okay." Caleb followed reluctantly.

"Hi, Caleb," Rachel said. "Is this your brother?" She closed her math book and moved her other books out of the way.

"Yeah. This is my brother Cole." Caleb put his stuff down and took the chair at the end of the table.

I put my backpack on the floor and sat between Rachel and Caleb. "We're waiting for our uncle to come pick us up. Thanks for the seat."

"Hey, are you the boys who caught the puppy that ran away from the pet store? That was really a wild chase. She ran right past me." Rachel pushed a stray strand of hair back into her clip.

"Uh huh." I nodded my head as I rummaged through my backpack to see if I had any money left from lunch.

"The puppies are real cute but I like kittens best. I used to have a Persian kitten before..." She left the sentence unfinished.

I pulled out two dollars from the backpack. I had 50 cents in my pocket.

"Caleb, do you have any lunch money left?"

Caleb put his hand in his pocket and pulled out a dollar bill. "This is all," he said.

"Good," I said and took the dollar. This should be enough to get us all some Cokes. It might take a little while for Uncle Bobby to get here. He has been known to get distracted." I exchanged glances with Caleb, who grinned and nodded his head.

"Our Uncle Bobby is great but he has his own ways of doing things." Caleb seemed to be getting more comfortable with Rachel.

"I'll go get the Cokes," I said, adding his money to mine.

"Get me a Dr. Pepper," said Caleb.

"Okay. What would you like to have Rachel?" I asked.

"Oh, you don't have to buy me a drink," she said, shyly.

"I have enough money for all three of us and you were nice enough to let us sit with you. I'll get you a soda." I stood up and looked around for the best place to get the drinks.

Rachel smiled. "Okay," she said. "I would like a Dr. Pepper too please."

"Good." I turned to Cole. "You better come with me to help carry the drinks."

When we got back to the table with the sodas, Rachel was working on her math again. "How can you work with all of this noise?" I looked around the packed mall.

"I am used to it," she said. She took a sip of her Dr. Pepper. "My mother works at the Dos Senoritas Mexican Restaurant at the north end of the mall. She doesn't get off work until it closes at 9:30. I come over here after school and do my homework here in the food court."

"Oh. It must be fun to hang out at the mall every day," I said.

Rachel shrugged her shoulders and took another sip of her drink. "It's okay."

Caleb took out his spelling book and turned to his list of words. He put the book up in front of him so he wouldn't have to talk to Rachel.

I really didn't want to take out all my homework. "I like to look at the puppies," I said. "My Mom told me not to ask Uncle Bobby to buy me anything for Christmas, but I just had to ask him if he would get me a puppy. It's all I really want."

"Why do you have to ask your uncle? Do you live with him?"

"Our mom and dad are traveling in Europe. After Christmas, they are going to Egypt."

"They're going to be gone a long time," Caleb added, from behind his spelling book.

I nodded my head and slurped some more coke. "They're photographers and work for the World Geographic magazine. They travel all over the world.

When they're gone, our Uncle Bobby comes and stays at our house and takes care of us."

"That must be hard, not seeing your mom and dad."

I nodded. "We talk with them several times a week by video conference. We get neat stuff from all over the world too. I miss them a lot at Christmas. They're usually home then. But it's a real long job this time. They won't get to come home until spring. They said they would get to stay home for six months then. I'm looking forward to that. They will be home for summer vacation."

"Do you think you will get a puppy?"

I thought about it a little before I answered. "I don't really know. I'm going to tell Mom and Dad when I talk with them later tonight that I asked for a puppy."

"There you are," said Uncle Bobby. He weaved his way through the crowd of people and packages and pulled up a chair to join us.

"You boys should be more careful of your time and not let it get dark before you start home. You know the rules," he said, sternly. "Especially this close to

Christmas. You don't want to be on Santa's bad-boy list, do you?"

Caleb quickly packed up his spelling. "I was ready to come home after the game store, but Cole had to go look at the puppies. Then one of the puppies got loose in the mall and we helped to catch her." Caleb told the story without stopping to take a breath. "It was a long chase," he finished.

"Did you catch her?" Uncle Bobby asked.

"I did," I answered. "It was a golden retriever puppy. It ran all over and then when she got tired, she ran straight to me. Golden retrievers are really good dogs from what I read on the Internet. Since you're here, could we go look at her again?"

Uncle Bobby shook his head. We need to get home because your mom and dad are going to call, remember?"

I frowned but nodded and picked up my soda trash and put it in the garbage can next to our table.

Uncle Bobby looked over at Rachel. "And who is this young lady?" he asked.

"I'm Rachel," she said. I'm in school with Caleb."

"Did you get involved in the great puppy chase?"

"No. I like kittens," Rachel replied, softly.

Uncle Bobby stood up. "Well, we better get on home. We will pick up some burgers on the way. How does that sound?"

"Great," I said, picking up my backpack.

"Rachel," Uncle Bobby said, "you can come over and play with the boys anytime you want. Okay?"

Caleb grabbed Uncle Bobby's hand. "Come on, we don't want to be late to talk to Mom and Dad."

I waved good-bye to Rachel. "Guess I'll see you around if you hang out here a lot."

Rachel waved back, and then went back to work on her math. I noticed as we turned to leave, her jeans were wrinkled too.

Chapter 4

Christmas Morning

"Cole, wake up! Wake up!"

I rolled over and squinted at Caleb. The sun was already beginning to come up at the window behind me. I groaned. Caleb was shaking me. What was he saying?

"Get up. It's *Christmas!* I looked downstairs just now. I can see all kinds of packages under the tree and one of them is *moving*! Hurry up!"

What Caleb was saying finally got through my sleepy brain. "Moving?"

"Yeah. Moving! Come on!" Caleb turned and ran in his bare feet and pajamas toward the stairs.

"Moving!" I repeated and scrambled out of bed. I thought about finding my robe, but I abandoned the idea as I ran to catch up with Caleb.

At the top of the stairs, I looked down into the living room. Packages were all around the tree. A large silver box, with a big, red bow on top, was scooting all over the hardwood floor.

I heard Uncle Bobby laughing. "WOOH HOO - What a Christmas morning! No Caleb, leave that box for Cole. Cole, come on down here. It looks like you got something really good!"

I took the stairs as fast as I could, missing the last one completely. I landed with a thud close to Uncle Bobby's chair. He sat down his mug of coffee on the end table and held out his hand. "No need to hurt yourself. You better get that box off of whatever that is pretty quickly, or there won't be a box left," he laughed again.

"Yeah, Cole. Take the top off. Hey! There it goes scooting toward the kitchen!" Caleb went around on the other side of the box and blocked its path.

I quickly recovered from my fall and caught up with the box. Or, it caught up with me. It had changed directions after running into Caleb. Now it was banging against my legs. I grabbed the box top - there wasn't a bottom - and pulled it up to free what was underneath.

I froze.

Caleb froze.

The grin on my face froze.

"Well, what do you think?" Uncle Bobby finally asked, chuckling. "Quite a surprise, I'd say!" He took another drink from his coffee mug.

Free of the box, "it" was sniffing at my feet.

Caleb started laughing. He didn't even go for his presents. He just sat down on the floor, rocking back and forth, laughing and pointing.

I felt something cold on my bare feet and jumped back. "Hey you, get your nose off my toes!" I am surprised I even managed to say that much.

Caleb laughed even harder. "It isn't a nose, Cole. It's a snout!" Caleb was rolling on the floor now. He was laughing so hard tears were running down his face. Finally, he got control long enough to call to it. "Here, piggy piggy! Come here, little piggy." The little pinkish thing with black splotches on his back ignored Caleb and followed me as I backed up.

Caleb started laughing again. "What's the matter, Cole? Don't you like your new pet?"

"He is a pot-bellied piglet, to be precise," Uncle Bobby explained, with pride. "Cynthia says a pig is a way better gift than a puppy. No one else in your class will likely have one." He drank some more coffee. "I checked with the city. They said it was okay to have a pot-bellied pig."

"No, I don't think anyone in my class will have one of these," I said, shaking my head.

Uncle Bobby nodded and continued talking about his girlfriend Cynthia. "Yes, she saw on TV where they make great pets. Some famous movie stars have them. Cynthia keeps up with stuff like that," he said, looking at his watch. "She should be here pretty soon to cook Christmas dinner. Be sure to thank her now. It was her idea." Uncle Bobby picked up the pig and rubbed its head. "You better finish opening your other presents before Cynthia gets here."

Caleb crawled under the tree and started opening his gifts. I got down on the floor and joined him. I couldn't help wondering what I was going to do with a pig. You can't even play ball with a pig!

Chapter 5

Christmas Afternoon

Cynthia fixed a very nice Christmas dinner. I mostly ate and avoided looking at her or anyone else. She brought me a collar and a leash for the pig. I really didn't know what to say, so I just said, "thanks."

After dinner, Cynthia took her camera from her purse. "Come on, let's take some pictures with the piglet," she said.

Uncle Bobby grinned. "He sure is a dandy gift, isn't he, Cole?"

Before I could think of a reply, Cynthia asked an even worse question, "Cole, what are you going to name him?"

I frowned. "I haven't really thought about it," I said.

I looked at the piglet and then back at Cynthia and grinned. "What about calling him 'Dandy' since he was such a 'dandy' gift?" I thought that would make her happy. There is a lot to be said for keeping girls happy.

"What about 'Dandy Danny'?" Caleb said, picking the piglet up and shoving him at me. 'Danny' was the name of Grandpa's old hound dog. Caleb was grinning from ear to ear.

"Oh, I like that, Caleb," Cynthia said. She took my arm and pulled me around to sit on the couch with the piglet in my lap. "There, that will make a nice photo."

CLICK CLICK went the camera. Then, CLICK CLICK some more...

How can I get out of here, I wondered? Then I saw the leash on the coffee table.

"Cynthia, don't you think it's time I took him out for a walk? We shouldn't just turn him loose in the backyard. Mom wouldn't like it if he tore up her roses."

"That is a great idea. Don't you think so, Bobby?"

Uncle Bobby nodded. "Why don't you take and show him off around the neighborhood."

As soon as Uncle Bobby shut the front door, I headed to a side street away from our neighborhood.

It was gray and cloudy. We just wandered around for a while. The air was crisp and cold. There was no wind, though, so I took my cap off and tried to think. When I put my cap in my pocket, I found a package of peanut butter crackers I had bought in the school vending machine. I didn't have time to eat them before the bell rang. I popped one in my mouth.

Dandy sniffed the air, smelling the peanut butter. I bent down and gave him one. "I guess you could have a cracker just this one time. After all, it is Christmas and you ate all the pig food Cynthia brought."

Dandy pushed the peanut butter cracker around a little, smelling it real good. He nibbled at it. He nibbled some more, then there were some crunching noises and the cracker was gone. He sat down and burped. He looked up at me and grunted.

"Oh you liked that did you?" I asked. "Well, no more right now. Maybe later. I put the rest of the crackers back in the pocket of my jacket

Dandy grunted again. Then he got up and snuffled around some leaves in the ditch by the side of the road. I pulled him away and started down the road again. He walked pretty well with me. I just had to set the direction. He didn't even pull the leash hard.

I shook my head as I stared at Dandy. I can't believe I got a pig instead of a puppy. That puppy at the mall sure was frisky. I bet she would play ball with me.

I kicked at a stick in the road. Dandy grunted and tried to investigate but I led him on.

The mall? I bet no one is there today because the stores aren't open on Christmas. I could walk over in the parking lot with Dandy and I wouldn't run into any of the boys from school. "Let's go, Dandy," I said, as I walked faster.

The mall parking lot was empty except for a big travel trailer at the far end of the mall behind the Mexican restaurant where Rachel's mother works. There was also a black pickup truck parked near the mall entrance.

I paused to zip up my jacket. It was cold, even if there wasn't any wind. I decided to check out the trailer. It was a funny place for a trailer to be parked. I wonder if someone is trying to steal stuff out of the restaurant, I thought.

When we got closer, I could see someone sitting on the step to the trailer.

I approached cautiously at first, and then I paused. "Hey Dandy, that looks like Rachel," I said. I kept walking and waved at her. I didn't think she would mind if I had a pig with me. "I wonder why she is at the trailer?" I said, more to myself than to Dandy. Rachel saw me but just stared and didn't wave back.

Before I could wonder why Rachel hadn't waved, Dandy squealed and pulled on the leash. From somewhere back toward the main part of the mall, I heard barking. It sounded like 'puppy' bark, not big dog bark.

"Come back here you, little stinker!" A man yelled from far behind me.

I recognized the voice of the pet store manager. I held on tightly to Dandy's leash and turned around as much as I could.

There, racing toward me at full speed across the parking lot, was a little red-gold ball of fur. It was the puppy from the Dog House! The very same one I had chased all over the mall! She was barking her heart out and running as fast as she could toward us. A blue leash dragged behind her. And behind that, the pet store manager ran but not nearly as fast as the puppy. He was way behind.

"Woof! Woof! Woof!"

Dandy squealed again and pulled harder at the leash. "It's Okay, Dandy," I said. I went down on one knee to pick him up so the puppy couldn't bother him. But Dandy was scared. He wiggled and squirmed and pulled the leash out of my hand. I fell on the cold asphalt, scraping my hand. Dandy was loose and running away too!

"Woof! Woof! Woof!" The puppy wasn't far away now.

"Oh, no! Stop, Dandy!" I shouted. He was headed toward the trailer as fast as his little legs could go.

I ran after Dandy but he had a good start on me. The puppy was close enough that I could hear her panting in between barks but I didn't look back. I had to catch Dandy.

Rachel was standing by the trailer now. I could see she was holding a stuffed animal of some kind.

"Stop him, Rachel!" I called.

Rachel carefully put the stuffed toy on the top step of the trailer and ran to head off Dandy. She squatted down and put out her hands. Dandy scooted past her and ran under the trailer. He hid behind one of the big wheels.

I slowed down and thought what I needed to do now was catch the puppy before she could get to Dandy. I stopped and whirled around just as the puppy ran past me. I turned back to run again and saw she had stopped and was sniffing at the edge of the trailer.

Rachel was walking quietly towards her. The puppy heard her and looked up, ready to scoot under the trailer too.

I walked slowly so I wouldn't scare her. I remembered the peanut butter crackers in my pocket.

"Here, puppy," I called. I waved the crackers in the air to get her attention so she could smell them. "I have a nice treat for you." I bent down and held the crackers out. "You have to come over here to get them."

The puppy turned toward me and took a step, but no more than that. She sniffed at the crackers but was still just out of my reach.

"Come on, girl. You know you want them," I said. I slipped one of the crackers out of the package and tossed it between us. She trotted to the cracker. She sniffed at it. Then she looked up at me to make sure I wasn't going to try to catch her. I thought I would wait until she was eating the cracker but she grabbed it and ran.

Luckily, she ran right into Rachel's arms.

"Gotcha!" The puppy wiggled but Rachel held her close.

"–Hey, that was teamwork," the pet store manager said. He was standing a few feet away with his hands on his knees trying to catch his breath and talk at the same time.

"That little puppy has caused me a lot of trouble."

The puppy whined and settled down in Rachel's arms. She licked at her ear.

I turned to the store manager. "Are you open today?" I asked.

He shook his head. "I still have to come and feed and walk the dogs, even when the store is not open. I usually pay my helper to do it. He quit after this little girl got loose in the mall." He pointed to the puppy snuggling in Rachel's care.

He shook his head again. His breathing was easier. "She has a lot of energy, and needs a lot of exercise."

"Well, looks like she got her exercise today," I said. I went over and patted her. "She sure is pretty," I said. She licked my fingers.

"Yes, she is a beauty," he said. "My name is Tom Morris. I own the Dog House. Say, you look like the boy who helped me catch her when she got loose in the mall."

"Yes, I'm Cole Jackson. I live down Peachtree Road, not far from here. I love dogs," I said. I scratched behind the puppy's chin.

"Mr. Morris, how much does this puppy cost?" I asked.

"Well, I was asking six hundred dollars for her. I thought a lady was going to buy her before Christmas. After we had to chase her down, she decided the puppy was too much for her to handle."

"Wow, that is a lot of money," I said.

Mr. Morris looked at the puppy and then back at me. "Tell you what," he said. "I'll let you have her for five hundred dollars since she didn't sell at Christmas."

I looked down and shook my head to hide my disappointment. "My parents can't afford to pay that much money," I replied.

I patted the puppy again as she squirmed in Rachel's arms. "I bet you're worth every penny. I wish I could take you home, but I can't," I told her.

Crunch. Crunch. Crunch.

Woof! Woof! Woof!

The puppy scrambled, trying to get down again. I helped Rachel hold on to her.

"What is that?" Mr. Morris asked, pointing.

I looked in the direction of the crunching noises and saw that Dandy was now out from under the trailer. He was crunching happily on the peanut butter cracker the puppy had dropped.

"That," I said, grinning, "is Dandy Danny, my pot-bellied pig." I could not help enjoy the look on Mr. Morris' face.

"You didn't get your puppy for Christmas?" asked Rachel.

I shook my head and sighed, trying to make the best of it. "I got Dandy Danny here," I admitted. I reached down and grabbed Dandy's leash so we wouldn't have to chase him down again.

"Oh, my," said Mr. Morris, "that is a really different kind of pet all right."

"It sure is." I shook my head like I did every time I thought about it. "You can't play ball with a pig." A pig doesn't make a very good best friend either, I thought, but didn't say that out loud.

"Well," said Mr. Morris, "some folks like 'em as pets just fine. I guess it depends on exactly what you're looking for."

"I guess," I said, politely.

Rachel handed the puppy to Mr. Morris.

"What about you? Do you like puppies?" he asked Rachel.

Rachel looked down at the parking lot. "I like kittens," she said. It was the same sad voice she had used to reply to Uncle Bobby when we were at the mall.

"Have a Merry Christmas," Mr. Morris said. He headed back toward the main mall entrance.

But he only got a few steps away before he turned and came back.

"Say, Cole." Mr. Morris was grinning and his eyes were shining. "You seem to be good with dogs. How would you like to work for me three days a week after school from four until six, and then from ten until two in the afternoon on Saturday? I could only pay you minimum wage. You could save your money, though, to buy this golden retriever, or some other puppy maybe."

I was speechless. Somewhere in the back of my mind, though, I heard my breath suck in.

Mr. Morris continued, "As I said before, I lost my assistant. There would be a lot of work. You would have to help feed the dogs and clean out the kennels. You would have to take them out for exercise and check them over each day to make sure they're all healthy." He paused, still smiling. "What do you say, Cole?" he said. Everybody deserves a chance to have a puppy." He looked at Dandy. "Even if he already has a pig."

It's funny how a perfectly bad day can turn into a perfectly good day. I could hardly keep from jumping up and down. "Oh, Mr. Morris, I would work really hard. I love being with the puppies and would take care of them really good. But I have to get permission first."

Mr. Morris nodded. "You ask your folks. Come by the Dog House tomorrow and let me know."

"Yes, sir," I replied and picked up Dandy. "I'll be over in the morning to let you know."

Mr. Morris frowned. "But, son, I want you to understand something. If somebody wants to buy this pretty little puppy before you're ready to buy her, I have to sell her. That is just the way business works." The puppy whined. He put her down and wrapped the leash around his hand so she couldn't pull away.

I swallowed hard and said, "I understand, Mr. Morris. I still want to work."

He smiled again. "Good. Merry Christmas. I'll see you tomorrow." He waved and tugged on the leash until the red-gold ball of fur was walking with him back to the mall. The puppy's tail waved like a red flag.

"What is going on out here?" The door to the travel trailer opened. Out of the corner of my eye, I saw the stuffed animal Rachel had left on the step go flying off onto the asphalt.

A tall lady with dark hair stood on the step where the stuffed animal had been.

Chapter 6

Hot Chocolate

"My kitten!" Rachel ran and picked up the stuffed animal. She brushed it off and held it close to her. She rocked it back and forth like a baby.

"Oh, I'm sorry honey. I didn't know you left her there," the lady said. Then she turned to me. "I thought I heard voices. Is this a friend of yours, Rachel?" She asked.

Rachel was calm now. "Mama, this is Cole. He was the boy who caught the puppy in the mall. Remember, I told you about the chase?"

"Oh, yes. What have you there in your arms, young man? A puppy?"

She must need glasses, I thought. Dandy grunted and wiggled in my arms. "No, Ma'am. It's a piglet." I sighed. I guess I had better get used to the questions, I thought.

"Oh, so I see." She patted Dandy on the head.

"I'm sorry we woke you up from your nap, Mama." Rachel came over and patted Dandy too.

"That's all right, honey. I needed to get up anyway," she said, and then shivered. "Would you kids like some hot chocolate? It feels like it is getting colder out here."

Rachel must live here in this travel trailer, I thought. I looked at the time on my Scooby-Do watch. It was five minutes past two. I needed to be home at four. Mom and Dad said they would call at 4:00 our time. They were in London, so that would be 10:00 at night London time. London is six hours later because of how the earth turns.

A little blast of wind came out of nowhere. Hot chocolate would sure be good before I walk home, I thought. "I need to call home and make sure it is okay," I said.

The lady pulled a cell phone from her pocket and handed it to me. "I'll go start the hot chocolate. I think I can find some marshmallows too," she said. She smacked her lips. "I think I am glad I woke up." She smiled and went back inside. I called Uncle Bobby.

When I finished, I handed the phone to Rachel. "Uncle Bobby said it was okay but I need to leave in about an hour," I said. I looked at the trailer more closely. "Do you really live here?" I asked.

She nodded and looked a little sad again. "My dad died in the war in Iraq and we had to move out of our house. I miss my Dad a lot. This is the first Christmas without him."

I put Dandy down but held on to the leash. "Oh, I'm sorry, Rachel." I didn't know what to say.

"Come on," she said. She grabbed my hand and pulled me toward the door. "I love hot chocolate. I could drink it all day long."

We sat at the little counter in the trailer, drinking hot chocolate. It was really good. I punched down some melted marshmallows with my spoon. Rachel's mother put Dandy in the bathroom so he wouldn't cause any more trouble. I could hear him rooting around.

"You kids enjoy your hot chocolate. I have some clothes to fold back in the bedroom," she sighed. "I wish we had more room to hang up our clothes." She went into the little bedroom and left us alone.

So, that was why Rachel's clothes were wrinkled. She has no place to hang them up!

Rachel pulled her kitten closer after her mother left the room. "It really is okay, you know," she said.

"What is?"

"Living here." She took a big drink of hot chocolate. It left chocolate all around her mouth. She licked it off.

"The man who owns the Dos Senoritas lets us connect to his electricity and water. He also gives us one meal a day. I never get tired of Mexican food." She paused. "My grandmother said we can come live with her out in California, but we have to save enough money to travel and to move our stuff out there. Mama put most of our stuff in a storage unit."

"Did you have a good Christmas?" I asked.

She nodded and drank more hot chocolate. She stuck out one foot. Mama gave me some knew tennis shoes, my grandmother sent me a new coat, and Santa gave me my kitty." She held the stuffed animal up for me to see. "Daddy gave me a real Persian kitten before he went to Iraq. We had to give her away when we moved. I called her Miss Priss." She looked a little sad again but continued.

"And last night, Mama read the Christmas story from the Bible about how baby Jesus was born in a stable. Then she read from the Gospel of John, chapter three, verse sixteen." She paused. "She always does that. She never reads about the baby Jesus without also reading the other verse." She paused again to drink her hot chocolate.

"What does the other verse say?" I asked.

I can't repeat it exactly but it says how much God loves us. It tells us that the reason he sent his son - that's the baby Jesus - is so if we believe on him, we will always have life. I know my Daddy believed and he is with God right now. Someday, I will be too."

I stirred my hot chocolate and thought about it. "I'm not sure I understand," I said.

Rachel put her cup on the counter and leaned forward. In almost a whisper, she said, "Daddy explained it to me this way. You know how when you do something bad at school, and you know your favorite teacher will be angry or disappointed in you?"

I nodded.

"Well, you don't feel like talking to the teacher then do you? You feel guilty?"

I nodded again and Rachel leaned back. "Well, it's kind of like that. When people do things against what God wants them to do, it makes God sad and keeps them from talking to him or being close to him. He wants us to be close to him where he can love and take care of us. He allowed his son, Jesus to be punished for what we do wrong."

"Like, if I took punishment for something Caleb did?"

"Yeah, like that. He loves us that much. It was the reason Jesus was born. He died for us and then came back from death. If we believe in Jesus and ask him to come into our hearts, we will always be close to God. No matter where we go or what happens to us, even after we die." Rachel sat back and drained the last of her hot chocolate.

"I never heard it explained that way before," I said. I thought about how hard it would be to be punished for something Caleb did. Pretty hard, I thought.

"Because of Jesus, we can be with God forever." Rachel grinned and picked up her stuffed kitty. She looked at her empty hot chocolate mug and sighed. "It's kind of like having hot chocolate all the time."

I smiled as I finished off mine. "Hot chocolate in your heart? All the time? Cool!"

Rachel giggled. I looked at my Scooby watch again and saw it was time to go. I heard Dandy Danny grunting at the bathroom door. "I have to go home now. Thank your Mom for the hot chocolate for me." I freed Dandy and took hold of his leash.

"Sure," she said and got up and walked with me to the door. "I hope your mom and dad let you work at the pet store."

"Me, too! See you around. Merry Christmas!" I waved and took off at a trot and focused on my plan to get that red-gold puppy.

Chapter 7

Figuring

I dumped a jar full of coins on the floor, where I already had several stacks of quarters, nickels and dimes.

"What are you doing?" Caleb asked.

I looked up to see Caleb coming into my room carrying Dandy in his arms.

"I am trying to figure out how much money I have, and how long I will have to work to buy that puppy. She will also need stuff like a dog bed, collar and leash. I'll have to figure those costs out, too."

Dandy grunted and squirmed. Caleb let him down on the floor.

"Hey, catch him." I pointed to Dandy. "I don't want to have to start counting all over again!" I said. But it was too late. Dandy had already knocked over three stacks of coins and scooted under the bed.

"I'll get him," Caleb said. He crawled under the bed and pulled him out. "Sorry. I'll put him in his kennel in the utility room." He paused. "Hey, did Mom say you could work in the Dog House for real?"

I scooped the coins into a pile and started over, separating out the quarters first. "Yes. She said if I really wanted the puppy and was willing to work for her, then it was okay. She thinks it would be good for me to work until school lets out for the summer," I said, without looking up.

"Even, after you buy the puppy?" Caleb asked.

"Yes." I looked up. "She said if I took a job, then I had to take it long enough to help Mr. Morris, not just long enough to get what I wanted."

"What about baseball?"

I shook my head. I had already thought about missing out on baseball after school. "The puppy is more important than baseball."

Caleb looked funny. "Wow! You must really want that puppy," he said.

"Yes. I have been reading about golden retrievers. They're supposed to make great 'best friends'. They are friendly with everybody, have lots of energy. They're smart too. Golden retrievers are often used for service dogs." I went back to my counting.

"What about me?" Caleb asked.

"What about you," I replied.

"Aren't I your best friend anymore?"

I stopped counting again and stood up. I put my hands on Caleb's shoulders. "Caleb, you are my brother, and we will always be the closest. But you and I like to do different things sometimes. I want a companion who will always be with me. No matter what I want to do. Do you understand what I mean?"

Caleb thought about it a bit, and then smiled. "Yeah, I think so. I guess you can play with that puppy when I want to play video games."

I nodded and tried again to go back to counting. Caleb still stood there holding Dandy. "What?" I asked.

"Aren't you forgetting about something in your grand plan?"

"What am I forgetting?" I asked. "It's all worked out. Uncle Bobby said he would pick me up at the mall after I finish work at the Dog House. He thought it was a great idea."

Caleb smiled. "What about Dandy here?" He lifted Dandy up and down in his arms. "You are supposed to feed him and take him for a walk after school. Who is going to do that?"

Uh oh. "I forgot about that," I groaned.

Caleb was still smiling. "Well, since we're still brothers, I suppose I could do it for you." He looked at the money I was counting. "For a price," he finished, and grinned.

I groaned again. "How much money do you want?"

"Hmmm…," Caleb thought, "I think ten dollars a week should be about right, don't you think?"

I gave him a long stare. "Well," I said, "it would solve the problem, but you'll have to promise you will do it every day I am working."

"You got a deal," Caleb said and held out his hand.

"Deal," I said, giving his hand one firm shake.

Chapter 8

First Day on the Job

"...and you will need to give each puppy a good walk. Puppies need a lot of exercise. There is a back entrance to the store through the storeroom. You can take them out to the parking lot through there," Mr. Morris said, pointing to the back exit.

"Okay," I said. "How many dogs do you have here in the store?"

"Right now, I have eleven," he said. "I'll introduce you."

We walked into the glassed-in kennel area.

"Woof! Yip! Yip! Grr!" There was a lot of noise from the puppies.

"Here," he said, and pointed to a small puppy with lots of long gray and white hair. The hair even fell over his face. He shook his head so the hair fell away from his eyes enough to see us. "This is a Lhasa Apso," Mr. Morris continued. "He won't get very big. I am calling him Flopsy because of all that hair flopping around." He moved on to the next kennel.

"This is Hamlet. He is a Russian Wolfhound." Mr. Morris continued down the line of kennels naming each dog. There were Stormy the Siberian Husky, Jamie the Collie, Ruby the chocolate Labrador, Sable the Newfoundland, Happy the cocker spaniel, Frenchie the Poodle, Oreo the Dalmatian, and Mutley the Snoodle.

"I never heard of a Snoodle before," I said.

"It's a cross between a Poodle and a Schnauzer."

"WOOOOOOOOOOH!"

"WOOOOOOOOOOOOOOH!"

We came to the last kennel. Mr. Morris tapped the front glass. The red-gold puppy put her paws on the glass and whined. She wanted out of the cage.

"And this young lady is Scarlet. I think you have met her a couple of times already," Mr. Morris said and grinned at me.

"WOOOOOOOOOOH," the puppy continued to howl. She wanted out!

"I call her Scarlet because of her red color." He pointed to her ears.

I remembered the word 'scarlet' from reading class. It means bright red. It was a good name for her, I thought.

"See how much darker red her ears are?" he said.

I nodded. Even though Scarlet was already red-gold all over, her ears were even redder.

"Well, you can tell what color a golden retriever will be when full grown by looking at the color of the puppy's ears. Scarlet is going to be very red when she grows up."

"WOOOOOOOOOOOOOOOOOOOOOOOOOOOO OOOOH!" Scarlet was ready to play!

Mr. Morris laughed. "She does like to howl. I guess you better start with her." He opened the kennel door and handed her to me.

Before I could do anything else, though, someone came in the store. All the dogs started barking. I wasn't sure what was going on. I knew from experience to hang on tight to Scarlet!

Chapter 9

Kittens in the Dog House

"Hey, is anyone here?" A man stood in front of the counter carrying a big cardboard box.

"Yes, here we are," Mr. Morris said and we came out from the kennel area. "Can I help you?" Mr. Morris asked.

"Meow, Meow," cries were coming from the box.

"I was wondering if you could take my kittens to sell?" he asked. "They are Persian kittens and I brought their papers with me."

"GRRRRRRR..." It was a soft grrrrrrrr.

"Shush, Scarlet. Those kittens won't be any fun for you to play with," I told her. "They would just scratch you."

Mr. Morris went over and looked in the box and took out one of the three kittens. "Well, I usually just sell dogs," he said. He held the kitten up and looked at him.

"They're all healthy," said the man, as he put the box on the counter. Two other little kitten heads popped up over the top of the box. One was gray and white, like the one Mr. Morris was holding. The last one was black, white and orange.

"I suppose I could do it this once," said Mr. Morris. He picked up the box. "Let's go in the office and talk."

"Come on, Scarlet, let's go find Rachel! She'll want to know about the kittens." I slipped the leash on the puppy and headed out the back door.

We found Rachel walking from the trailer toward the mall carrying her books. Her eyes lit up when I told her about the kittens. She was really excited.

"I have to walk all of the puppies now but you should go check the kittens out," I said.

"Thanks, Cole," she said. "I'll see you when you get through with your chores." She waved and ran toward the pet store.

Scarlet and I watched as Rachel hurried away, dropping one book and then another without noticing.

"I guess we better pick those up for her, huh, Scarlet?" I smiled. "Come on, girl. You and I finally get to spend some time together." I pulled a dog treat from my pocket. She gobbled it down and sniffed my hand for more treats.

I squatted and she put her paws on my knee. Then she jumped down and rolled over for me to rub her belly. "Now, this is the way it should be, Scarlet," I whispered. "Just the two of us. Best friends forever."

Chapter 10

Double Close Call

I loved working at the Dog House. I got to know all the dogs well. It was hard, though, to watch them go home with someone.

The Dalmatian went home with a little girl. The Newfoundland went home with a man who lived outside of town. He said he had plenty of room for Sable. He had two other Newfoundland dogs at home. He must spend a lot of money on dog food, I thought. Newfoundland puppies grow up to be huge dogs.

Rachel came to the pet store every day to play with the kittens. Her favorite was the three-colored one. She called it Miss Calico. 'Calico' is another name for a cat with three colors in her coat. Rachel said the kitten was like the one her daddy had given her before he went to fight in the war.

It was clear the kitten favored Rachel. When Rachel held her in her lap, she purred and purred.

Rachel was there the day 'the lady' came in.

I noticed the frown on Mr. Morris' face when the woman walked in the door and knew something was wrong. I still remember the purple scarf around her neck and the big black handbag she carried.

She walked over to the counter. "Mr. Morris, I am still thinking about that golden retriever puppy I saw before Christmas," she said. "Do you still have her?"

Rachel and I looked at each other. "Oh, no!" I cried. I ran and put the leash on Scarlet. "Let's go, girl," I said. "Let's go for a long walk." We hurried toward the back door but Mr. Morris stopped us.

"Here she is now," Mr. Morris told the lady.

I reluctantly led Scarlet back to the counter and lifted her up into the lady's arms.

"Whoa," said the lady. "You've really grown since I saw you at Christmas!"

The lady was right. Scarlet was much bigger now. Her coat was turning a darker red. It was soft and silky.

Scarlet wiggled her whole body and the woman almost dropped her.

"I can see you still have lots of energy," she said.

"Woof, woof," Scarlet replied. She sunk her teeth into the handles of the lady's leather purse and chewed.

"Stop it!" The lady swatted Scarlet on the nose. "Stop it!" she said. She let Scarlet drop to the floor but Scarlet pulled the purse down too.

"Oh, no! Give that back right now," the lady screamed.

All kinds of things fell out of the purse and clattered to the floor as Scarlet dragged it down the nearest aisle.

"Oh, you bad dog!" The lady ran after her purse and Scarlet.

I looked at Rachel. She was holding one of the gray kittens and grinning.

I almost grinned back but decided I better try to help catch Scarlet.

I followed the lady, picking up the scattered purse stuff as Scarlet rounded the corner of the aisle.

"I'll close the doors so she won't get out into the mall again," I heard Mr. Morris say.

The glass doors of the store slid shut with a rattle.

Scarlet was now at the front of the store near the counter. She stopped and gave the purse a good shake, flinging the last of its contents onto the floor.

"Give me that, you awful puppy!" The woman grabbed the bottom of the handbag and pulled. Scarlet held onto the handles and pulled back.

"Grrr...," Scarlet replied. This is some fun game; she must have been thinking.

The lady pulled harder.

Scarlet pulled harder.

The handles came away from the rest of the purse and the lady fell backward onto the floor.

"Oh, no," cried Mr. Morris. "Let me help you up." He hurried toward the lady, holding out his hand. "Are you hurt?" he asked.

Scarlet reached the lady before Mr. Morris did. She jumped into the lady's lap, knocking off her glasses as she tried to lick her face.

The lady pushed at her. Scarlet ignored the pushing and pulled the lady's purple scarf from her neck.

"Somebody get her off of me!" The lady was not happy. She pushed herself off the floor. I grabbed Scarlet's leash and pulled her away. I managed to wrestle the scarf away from Scarlet and handed it back.

"I am so sorry!" Mr. Morris took the lady's arm and helped her to the chair behind the counter. "The puppy just wanted to play," he explained.

Scarlet sat down by my side and tilted her head to one side. She didn't understand what all the fuss was about. She looked like a sweet puppy now.

I gathered up the rest of the lady's things and kept the leash around my wrist so Scarlet wouldn't get away again.

"Of course, I will pay for the damage," Mr. Morris said.

"Yes, you will," the lady replied, angrily. "You are lucky I didn't hurt myself."

Mr. Morris nodded.

Rachel came up to the counter still holding the kitten. The little gray kitten wiggled and meowed.

"What is that?" asked the lady, as she turned her head. "Oh, a kitten!" Her voice softened. "I didn't know you sold kittens."

Mr. Morris took the kitten from Rachel and handed it to the woman.

"I usually don't but I took on three Persians. I was asking three hundred for each. Since you had such a bad time today, I'll sell you one for a hundred dollars," Mr. Morris said.

"Hmm…," said the lady, as she played with the kitten. "You say you have three to pick from?"

"Yes," replied Mr. Morris. He turned to me.

"Cole, go get the other two kittens for us, please," he said, "and put Scarlet back in her kennel."

"Yes, sir," I said and hurried off with Scarlet close to my side. I noticed she was walking with me real nice now. But I didn't have time to think about that. I put her in her kennel and got the other two kittens.

"Well, I like the two gray kittens," said the lady, "but I don't want the three-colored one."

Rachel breathed a sigh of relief and quickly took the kitten from the lady's lap and hugged her.

"Will you sell me both gray kittens for one hundred dollars each?" the lady asked.

Mr. Morris sighed. "Okay," he said. "You have a deal."

The lady stood up and looked through the contents of her purse, now in a pile on the counter. "I just need to find my wallet so I can pay you."

"I walked over to Rachel and whispered, "That was way too close."

Rachel swallowed hard and said, sadly, "Yes, but my kitten will be sold sometime."

She stroked the three-colored kitten. It purred and purred again.

I frowned when she said "her kitten."

BAM! BAM! BAM!

"Open up! Open up!"

Caleb was at the closed glass door. His face was red from running and he was out of breath.

Mr. Morris opened the door. Caleb hurried past the lady as she left with the kittens and her broken purse in her arms.

"Cole, you have to come home right now! Uncle Bobby sent me to get you," he said.

"What's wrong?" I asked.

"The World Geographic magazine called. Mom and Dad have missed their last two check-in calls from Egypt. They are MISSING!"

Chapter 11

Waiting

I hate waiting. Mom says I am just like her about things like that. Dad says Mom and I need to learn patience. But patience is hard.

Uncle Bobby was watching the news when Caleb and I got home.

"Rioting in Egypt," the newsman said. I could see pictures of a crowd of angry men shouting in the streets.

"I'm glad you're home," Uncle Bobby said. "I have been calling your parents' cell phone all day and they didn't answer. The man from the magazine said the last they heard from them, they were in their hotel room. There was a mob of people outside the hotel. Some rocks had been thrown through the hotel windows."

"Grunt. Grunt. Grunt." Dandy Danny trotted up to the couch. Caleb picked him up.

"Caleb, you and Dandy seem to be getting along well," I said.

"Yeah. He follows me all around the house now. I like walking him when you're at work."

We watched the news for some time and then the doorbell rang.

"Go ahead and see who that is, Cole," Uncle Bobby said.

I opened the door and there stood Mr. Morris, with Scarlet sitting prettily beside him on the porch.

I opened the door to let them in.

"I came over to see if there was any news about your parents," he said. Scarlet jumped up to greet me. "Scarlet has been howling and howling ever since you left the store. I think she knows something is wrong."

I hugged Scarlet. She was alive with energy, happy now that she was with me.

Uncle Bobby stood up and shook Mr. Morris' hand. "Come on in. There isn't any word yet. The magazine said they would call as soon as they hear from them." He turned the sound down on the TV.

"I hope everything works out," Mr. Morris said. He pointed to Scarlet. "I thought Cole might like to have Scarlet spend the night with him if it is okay with you."

"Could she, really?" I pleaded. "I'll take good care of her."

"She has already had her supper but will need some water. Golden retrievers need a lot of water," he said. "You can bring her back to the store tomorrow when you come to work."

"Well, I guess it would be all right if she stays," replied Uncle Bobby.

"Can she sleep in my room? Please?" I asked.

"I guess so." Uncle Bobby smiled and sat back down in his chair.

"Can Dandy sleep with me?" Caleb asked.

I just remembered Dandy was on the couch and whirled around.

Sure enough. Scarlet had found him already. Her paws were on the couch and she was licking Dandy all over. Dandy seemed to like it!

I breathed a sigh of relief.

"I guess it is okay for tonight, boys. There are some sandwiches Cynthia made for you on the table in the kitchen. Why don't you take them upstairs with you? You can get on the computer and check if there's any email from your mom and dad. I checked earlier but it wouldn't hurt to check again."

Caleb and I took Scarlet, Dandy and the sandwiches to my room and checked email but there wasn't anything. I left the computer on so I could check again later.

When we finished our sandwiches, Caleb picked Dandy up. "I'm going to go to bed now. Let me know if you hear anything," he said.

"Okay," I said. I climbed up on the bed with Scarlet. She crawled into my lap or as much of her as she could get into my lap. She really had grown.

Caleb hesitated at the door. "Cole," he asked, "do you think God would hear prayers for Mom and Dad?"

I pulled the blinds up and looked out the window over my bed at the night sky. "God took care of Rachel and her mother, even when their house was lost. I think he would take care of Mom and Dad if we ask him."

"I am going to take Dandy Danny into my room and pray," he said and hurried out, shutting the door behind him.

I looked at Scarlet. She was almost asleep. I looked out at the dark night and prayed.

"Jesus, please come into my heart the way you are in Rachel's heart. Forgive me when I do things wrong. I want to be close to you always. I believe that because you took my punishment and overcame death, I can be with you forever, even in heaven someday.

I stroked Scarlet's soft fur. "Thank you for loving me enough to come and suffer for me," I continued, "and thank you for making dogs to be our special friends. Especially, this golden retriever here. I love her and need her a lot."

I bent down and hugged the snoring Scarlet tighter. "Please watch over Mom and Dad wherever they are," I continued. "Keep them safe and bring them back to us."
I laid my head on the pillow and dragged Scarlet up to the pillow. She didn't even wake up. She just stirred

enough to snuggle closer and put a paw over my arm. That was the last thing I remembered until I my alarm went off.

I rubbed my eyes. Scarlet stirred but didn't wake up. I had set the alarm early, even though it was Saturday morning. I climbed out of bed and went straight to the computer.

I blinked. I leaned closer to the screen just to be sure I was seeing it. There it was. A message with Mom and Dad's address! I double 'clicked' on it with the mouse and read:

"Safe in Greece. We had to leave all our stuff behind at the hotel, but we are okay. Flying out to London. We will call you from the London office. We are sending this email from a computer borrowed from a tourist at the airport. Love, Dad."

I wiped the tears from my eyes. The phone rang downstairs.

There was a mad scramble of boys, pig and puppy down the stairs.

Mom and Dad were staying in London for two weeks to wrap up their work. Then they would be coming home. They said they were looking forward to a nice long vacation at home. "Thank you, dear Jesus," I said, as I headed to the Dog House with Scarlet. I smiled. It wouldn't be long before I could bring Scarlet home with me to stay too. Maybe even by the time Mom and Dad got home.

I paused at the front of the Dog House. In the window was a big sign.

KITTEN FOR SALE. MARKED DOWN TO SEVENTY-FIVE DOLLARS!

Chapter 12

A Decision

"Good Morning, Mr. Morris," I said, as I put Scarlet in her kennel. "We heard from Mom and Dad. They're in London now. They'll be coming home in a couple of weeks."

"Oh, that is good news, Cole," he said, as he paused from wiping down the counter.

"I see you have put the last kitten on sale," I said.

"Yes, I want to get her sold to make room for another puppy I have coming in next week," he replied.

"Rachel sure will miss her," I said.

Mr. Morris frowned. "I know, but it can't be helped." He went behind the counter and opened the register for the day. "Don't let me forget to pay you for the week when you leave today." He looked up at me. "You must be getting close to having the money to buy Scarlet?" he asked.

"In two more weeks, I will have enough money," I said. "I have to pay my brother some money each week for walking Dandy."

Mr. Morris nodded. "I see." He smiled.

I took Stormy the Husky out of her kennel for her morning walk. Out in the parking lot, Rachel came running up.

"I have lots of news," she said, breathing hard.

"Did you hear that Mom and Dad are okay?" I asked, before she told me her news.

"Yes. I was walking down to your house this morning to see if there was any word from them. I ran into Caleb and Dandy. Caleb told me all about it. That's when it happened. Caleb was great!" she said.

I switched hands on the leash as Stormy explored a patch of grass and tree on the edge of the parking lot.

"What happened?" I asked.

"Tony saw us and came over and started teasing me. He called me some awful names. He even called Caleb 'pig boy', when he saw Dandy."

"What did Caleb do?" I asked.

"He told Tony that a 'real man' doesn't call anybody names, especially girls."

"Oh, and I guess you are a 'real man'? Tony said," Rachel continued the story.

"Then Billy showed up and I really got scared. Caleb could see I was scared and stood between me and them. He told Tony to leave us alone, that Tony wasn't perfect either. He reminded them about the fly ball Tony missed that cost them the game last week. Billy laughed at Tony and said he should go spend the day playing catch so they wouldn't lose another game." Rachel took a deep breath.

"What happened then?"

"Tony's face turned red. He said it was just a practice game. The season hasn't really started yet. Then he pulled Billy away and said they had better things to do than mess around with us. Then they left." Rachel was finished.

"Wow! I guess my little brother is growing up," I said, proudly. "I am glad you were not hurt."

"Me, too!"

I pulled on the leash and continued to walk the puppy. I had a lot of them to walk and I didn't want to waste too much time. After all, I was working.

Rachel followed me. "That isn't all the news," she said, as she caught up with me.

"What else?" I asked, as I turned the puppy back toward the mall.

"Mama said we have enough money saved to get our stuff and move out to California to live with my grandmother. We're going to leave next Saturday." She frowned, then continued. "I'll miss you and Caleb and Dandy and Scarlet," she said. "And I'll miss the kitten at the pet store." I could see she was about to cry.

"Maybe your grandmother will let you have a kitten when you get there," I said. I was trying to make her feel better.

"I already asked her. She said it would be okay. But, she doesn't know anyone around that has kittens and she doesn't have money to buy a kitten. Neither does my mom." She sighed. "I'll go back to the Dog House with you and play with Miss Calico while I can."

I finished walking the dogs and cleaning up. Then I took Scarlet out of her kennel to work with her on 'sitting', and 'staying'. She needed a lot of work on 'staying'. Rachel was at the back of the store with Miss Calico for the rest of the morning.

Scarlet sat by my side. I looked down the aisle at Rachel. I put my hand on Scarlet's head and she looked up at me. Then she looked at Rachel and whined.

I bent down to talk things over with Scarlet. "What do you think, girl? Can you wait a little longer to come home with me if I buy that kitten for Rachel?" I asked her.

Scarlet nuzzled me and then licked my face. "I don't know if I can do this or not, girl. I love you so much," I said. I put my arms around her. "I don't want to risk someone coming in and buying you before I can."

Scarlet stopped licking my face and looked at Rachel. She whined and cocked her head at me.

I wondered what Jesus would do? I remembered how much Jesus loved me and how he helped me. I knew I had to help Rachel. I hugged Scarlet again and looked into her brown eyes. "I promise I will keep working until

I get you. Just, as soon as I can." She put a paw up and I shook it. Scarlet knew she was my puppy, no matter what.

I wiped my eyes on the arm of my shirt and then went to the counter. Mr. Morris was smiling and hanging up the phone. "Guess what, Cole," he said. "The woman who bought the other two kittens decided she wants the last one. She is coming in tonight after work to buy her."

I lowered my head and then looked back up at Mr. Morris.

Mr. Morris frowned. "What's wrong, Cole?" he asked.

I took a deep breath and said, "Mr. Morris, would you sell me the kitten before that lady comes back?"

Mr. Morris looked surprised. "I thought you wanted Scarlet?"

"Oh, yes, I do, Mr. Morris," I answered. "I love her best of all. But Rachel is going away to live at her grandmother's house in California and I want her to have the kitten. I will work longer to buy Scarlet. As, long as it takes. Please, Mr. Morris," I said, "let me buy the kitten."

Mr. Morris looked down the aisle where Rachel was still busy playing. "I see," he said, thoughtfully, then smiled.

"I think that's a great idea. I will even give Rachel the rest of the cat food I have in the back, since this is my last kitten. Do you want me to apply this week's pay to the kitten?"

"Yes, sir," I said. I felt both relieved and numb at the same time.

Mr. Morris took a small pet carrier from the shelf behind the counter. "She'll need this, too," he said. "I'll make this my going-away present to her. I will miss her being in here every day."

Scarlet and I followed Mr. Morris to where Rachel was sitting on the floor with the kitten. Even though it was hard, I knew I had made the right decision.

"This fine young man has paid for Miss Calico here," Mr. Morris said. "I brought this carrier for you to take her to California in."

Rachel's mouth fell open as Scarlet and I came from around behind Mr. Morris.

"For real?" she asked, looking at me with wide eyes.

"Woof!" said Scarlet.

"For real," I answered.

She stood up, still holding the kitten. She looked happier than I had ever seen her look.

"I guess you are growing up, too." she said.

I shrugged.

"Thank you so much, Cole. I will never forget this - or you. I'll try to see you next Saturday morning before we leave for California."

Mr. Morris took Miss Calico from Rachel and put her in the pet carrier.

"Cole, I expect you and Scarlet better help Rachel get her kitten and cat food back to the travel trailer."

"Okay," I said."

"You mean you bought that kitten for Rachel?" asked Caleb.

"Yeah. It just seemed like the right thing to do. You know, like you stood up for Rachel this morning. That was the right thing to do, too. Mom and Dad will be proud of you Caleb." I sat on top of the bed counting what was left of my money. "I'll be glad when they come home."

"Me, too," said Caleb. He left the room and came back a few minutes later carrying his old money bag. Dandy Danny was right behind him. Caleb dumped his money on the bed with mine.

It was a lot of money. I looked up at him. "What is this?" I asked.

"I saved the money you gave me to walk Dandy and my birthday money. I was going to buy a new video game. I decided I want to buy Dandy from you, instead," he said.

Dandy grunted and Caleb picked him up and sat down on the other end of the bed. "He's a lot more fun than a video game."

I shook my head and smiled. "You don't have to buy Dandy," I said. "Dandy is yours anyway."

"I know," he said, patting Dandy's head. Caleb pulled him away after he tried to snuffle the money.

"But I want him to be really mine. And I want you to have enough money to buy Scarlet."

I looked at him for a minute. My heart was doing flip flops as I thought maybe I could buy Scarlet now. "Okay, Caleb. You now officially own Dandy Danny. Let's count and see if there is enough money to get Scarlet."

Chapter 13
Good-byes

I slammed my book closed and looked at the clock. It was almost time for the bell to ring and school to let out on Friday afternoon.

I had enough money to buy Scarlet. Uncle Bobby made me wait until this afternoon because all week we were taking state-required tests at school. It was hard to think about math and history when Scarlet was waiting for me.

The bell finally rang. I grabbed my books and headed out the door. Caleb and Rachel met me in front of the school. They were going to walk to the mall with me to get Scarlet.

"She is going to be all mine," I told Caleb. "Just like Dandy is yours. I won't have to take her back to the store anymore." I stopped and pulled a new collar and leash from my backpack. "Don't you think she will look nice in this blue collar?"

"She'll look just beautiful," Caleb agreed. "She'll be as pretty as those dogs in the dog show we watched on TV."

Rachel opened her bag and pulled out a little package wrapped in pink paper. "I have a brush for her. Her fur is getting long and thick now. You are going to need it."

"Thanks, Rachel." I took the brush and put it in my backpack. "She'll like that."

"Hey, look over there," Rachel said. "It's getting to be springtime! The tulips are blooming and there's a blue jay in that pine tree."

I looked up. Even one more reason to be happy, I thought. Scarlet and I can run and play in the backyard and in the park.

"It will be nice weather for your trip to California, Rachel," I said.

"We're leaving very early in the morning. I wrote down our phone number and address for you. I want you to call and tell me all about your fun with Scarlet."

Rachel's mother was waiting for us at the mall entrance. She looked upset. She waved to us.

"What is it, Mama?" asked Rachel, a bit alarmed.

"You children sit down here on the bench with me for a minute. I have something to tell you," she said.

"But I need to go get Scarlet," I replied.

"Sit down, Cole," she said, patting the bench.

We all sat down.

"I am so sorry, children, but the dogs are gone," she said.

"What do you mean the dogs are gone? I am supposed to get Scarlet today!"

"I am so sorry, Cole. This morning, some men came to the pet store and said Mr. Morris had to shut down because he owed the bank a lot of money. The sheriff came with all of the legal papers. They took everything out of the store, including the dogs."

"You mean they took the store like they took our house?" cried Rachel.

Rachel's mother nodded. "The mall owns the store space but the men took everything that was in the store.

Mr. Morris had a lot of stuff for dogs in there. I suppose they will re-sell it for the money he owes them."

"No!" I said. "They can't do that!"

Rachel's mother shook her head. "I am afraid they can," she said. "Mr. Morris tried to keep Scarlet back but the sheriff said Scarlet belonged to the bank."

"What are they going to do with the dogs?" I asked.

"I have been trying to find that out. I called the bank. Everything was turned over to an auction house. The auction house is run by someone way up in New York. They don't seem to know anything about the dogs. I am sorry, Cole."

"Where is Mr. Morris?"

"He told me he was going to go visit his son in Florida for a while, maybe even retire there. He was very upset, especially about the dogs."

I left my backpack on the bench and ran into the mall. This just can't be true. Scarlet is *my puppy*!

Rachel and Caleb followed me to the Dog House.

There was a legal-looking sign on the glass door and inside everything was gone, even the cash register.

"What is going to happen to her?" I cried. Tears were rolling down my face. I didn't care. I sat down on the floor.

People walking by stared at us.

Rachel was crying, too. "Let's ask God to take care of Scarlet and all of the other dogs," she said.

"Is a dog important to God?" asked Caleb.

Rachel nodded. "I know they are. He made dogs and cats to be our special companions. If he made them, he has to care about them."

"And pigs, too?" asked Caleb.

Rachel nodded. "Pigs, too," she answered.

"Okay," I said. "Let's pray for them all."

We joined hands and prayed for all of the puppies. We prayed that God would keep them safe and give them good homes where they would be loved. "And give Scarlet to someone very special," I added.

When we finished praying, Caleb said, "I think we better go home now, Cole. Dandy will need some walking."

I took a deep breath and nodded. Suddenly, I wanted to see Dandy too.

I turned to Rachel. "I guess this is good-bye to you if you're leaving early in the morning."

She pulled out a piece of paper from her notebook. "Here is our phone number like I said."

"I wish you could stay and meet our mom and dad next week. They're coming in next Saturday morning."

Rachel didn't reply.

"Let us know when you get to California, okay?" I said.

"Okay," she said, then hesitated. "Thanks for being my friends."

I nodded.

"You know, maybe you could find another dog at the dog shelter. People aren't the only ones who end up homeless."

I nodded again. I was too full of Scarlet's loss to think about any other puppy right now. I just wanted to go home and see Dandy.

Chapter 14

Perfect Puppy

I hugged Dad, while Caleb hugged Mom. "Oh, you've both grown so much," said Mom.

"Let's go get your bags. We don't have much time," said Uncle Bobby. "The plane was almost an hour late."

Dad looked at his watch. "We better come back to the airport later to get the bags," he said.

Mom looked at her watch. "You're right. We may not make it, even if we leave now," she said. "Let's go!"

I picked up Mom's carry-on case. "Why are we in such a hurry? Aren't we just going home?" I asked.

Dad shook his head. "We have a meeting to go to on the way home. It shouldn't take very long," he said.

"A meeting?" Caleb asked. "Now?"

"Yes and we just have to make it. It's very important," Mom said.

"Can we stop and get hamburgers first?" Caleb asked. "We haven't eaten lunch yet."

Mom and Dad looked at each other but kept walking fast. "Afterward," Dad said.

"Yes," said Mom. "Later, we will get a lot of hamburgers." She smiled at Dad.

That was a funny answer, I thought. "I just want one," I said.

"We could bring one home to Dandy," said Caleb.

"I can't wait to meet Dandy Danny," said Mom. We buckled up in Uncle Bobby's SUV.

The 'meeting' was across town in a big glass building. I don't know how many floors it had but it was real high. I thought Uncle Bobby, Caleb and I would have to wait in the SUV, but Mom told us to come with them.

We went up to the tenth floor to a huge room with rows and rows of chairs and lots and lots of people. Someone was at the front of the room talking. The meeting had already started.

We found seats on the far side of the room about midway down. Caleb and I were too short to see anything. Caleb took out his pocket video game and I watched him play.

"Do you have the listing?" I heard Dad ask Mom.

Mom pulled a folded paper from her purse. "Yes, it is number seventy-five in the list." She handed the paper to Dad.

"They're on item sixty-five now," said Uncle Bobby.

"I guess Mom and Dad are going to buy somebody's pictures, like they did last summer," I whispered to Caleb.

The video game Caleb was playing made a beeping sound and then said "Game Over." He handed it to me. "Here, you try," he said.

I had been playing a lot of video games since I lost Scarlet. I focused on the game.

I heard Dad bid on something but couldn't see over the crowd. Caleb stood up on his chair to see. "We might need to bring home another hamburger," he said. There was a big grin on his face.

"Huh?" I said. Another man bid.

Then I heard someone else, not the auctioneer, down front yell, "Whoa! Whoa! Hold on, now!"

I stood up on my chair as Dad bid again. Mom noticed us and said, "Sit down before you fall."

"Down! Sit! Sit! Down! Sit!" The man up front was yelling louder. Reluctantly, I jumped down from the chair.

"Ooof," said the man up front. I heard him hit the floor.

"Sold!" the auctioneer said. He was pointing in Dad's direction.

"Whooooooooooooooooooo! Whoooooooooooooo! Whoooooooo!"

"Catch her! She's loose!"

I saw a flash of red as it left the front stage.

I couldn't believe it! Could it really be true? "Scarlet!" I called. "Scarlet! Come! Come!"

People were standing now. Scarlet scooted around and under them.

Crash! Crash! And another crash! Chairs in the rows ahead were falling down.

Caleb reached in his pocket and handed me an open pack of peanut butter crackers. "Here, you might need these," he said.

I headed in the direction of the chaos. Dad followed me.

"Grab the leash," I heard a lady say.

"Oh, she is pretty but fast!" someone else said.

"Pretty, fast and strong! I can't hold her!" I heard another thud and crash as another chair hit the floor.

Then suddenly, there she was standing up on the chair in front of me with her paws on its back. "Woof," she barked, very softly. The chair fell backward on me and I went down.

I didn't care. My arms went around Scarlet. She licked my face and then ate the crackers.

I sat up and she squirmed into my lap. She was really too big to fit, but I didn't care.

"Oh, she is such a bad dog! I'm glad I didn't buy her," said the man who had bid against Dad.

Scarlet ignored him and nuzzled my ear. I kept my arms firmly around her and said to the man, happily,

"No, she isn't a bad dog, Mister. She's my perfect puppy!"

The End

Questions for Discussion

1. Do you have a pet? How is it special to you?

2. What do you think about the boys who were mean to Rachel? What can you do when you see someone being mean to someone else?

3. What has God done to show his love for you?

4. What can you do to help God take care of animals?

5. Have you ever done anything special for someone else? What can you do to help someone you know?

6. What do you think the Bible verse in the Gospel of John, Chapter 3, and Verse 16 means? (John. 3.16)

References / Works Cited

The Guide-To-God New Testament: Philadelphia, PA; National Bible Press for Baptist Publications Committee. 1971

CPSIA information can be obtained
at www.ICGtesting.com
Printed in the USA
LVOW13s1534080217
523626LV00009B/558/P